This Walker book
belongs to:

For Cal, with all Nana's love
C. D. S.

For Peter Tobia, "Grandad"
L. T.

First published 2014 by Walker Books Ltd
87 Vauxhall Walk, London SE11 5HJ

This edition published 2015

2 4 6 8 10 9 7 5 3 1

Text © 2014 Carol Diggory Shields
Illustrations © 2014 Lauren Tobia

The right of Carol Diggory Shields and Lauren Tobia to be identified as
author and illustrator respectively of this work has been asserted by them
in accordance with the Copyright, Designs and Patents Act 1988

This book has been typeset in Dodson

Printed in China

British Library Cataloguing in Publication Data:
a catalogue record for this book is available from the British Library

ISBN 978-1-4063-6004-2

www.walker.co.uk

BABY'S GOT THE BLUES

Carol Diggory Shields

illustrated by Lauren Tobia

WALKER BOOKS
AND SUBSIDIARIES
LONDON • BOSTON • SYDNEY • AUCKLAND

Let me tell you, that's a lie.
Sometimes being a baby
Is enough to make you cry,
'Cause I'm a baby,
And I've got those baby blues.

B-A-B-Y, baby,

Got the poor little baby blues.

Woke up this morning soggy,
And I didn't feel
    too happy.
But I can't talk,
    no way to say,

"Won't somebody change my nappy?"

'Cause I'm a baby,
Got those baby stinkeroos.

B-A-B-Y,
baby,

Got those damp old baby blues.

I'd like to eat some pizza,
Macaroni, or lamb stew,
But I haven't got a single tooth,

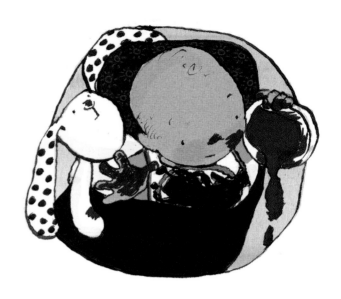

So I can't even chew.

I'm a baby,
And I never
get to choose.

B-A-B-Y,
baby,

I've got the
hungry baby blues.

I'm watching all the bigger kids—
They run and jump and race.
But every time I try to walk,

I fall flat on my face.

I'm a baby,
Can't even tie my shoes.

A B-A-B-Y,
baby,

With the goin'-nowhere
baby blues.

I'm a baby,
Paying my baby dues.

B-A-B-Y,
baby,

Got those locked-up
baby blues.

Sometimes I'm feeling low-down,
Snifflin', "Boo-hoo, boo-hoo-hoo."

Then someone scoops me up
With a "Cootchy-cootchy-coo!

B-A-B-Y, baby,

Don't you know
we all love you?"

And all those hugs and kisses
Make me lose those baby blues.

I'm a baby,
And I've lost those low-down blues,
A B-A-B-Y, baby,

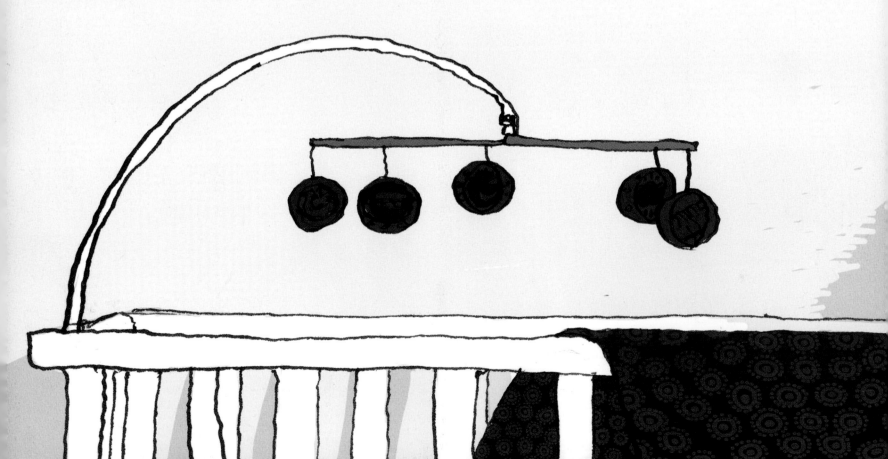

Cuddled up in I love yous.

Carol Diggory Shields is the author of more than twenty books for children, including *The Bugliest Bug* and *Saturday Night at the Dinosaur Stomp*, which she wrote after "being called a Nagosaurus by my five-year-old". It was time spent with her three baby grandchildren that inspired her to write *Baby's Got the Blues*. A children's librarian, she has also worked with children as a recreational therapist and a stuffed-toy designer. Carol lives in the USA, in northern California.

Lauren Tobia graduated from the University of the West of England with a degree in Illustration and was highly commended in the Macmillan Children's Book Prize. She went on to illustrate the Anna Hibiscus novels and picture books by Atinuke. Lauren says that illustrating *Baby's Got the Blues* transported her back to the time when her own children were young – and to her own childhood, when she was the big sister. Lauren lives in Bristol with her family.

Other books you might enjoy:

978-0-7445-9813-1   978-1-4063-1268-3   978-1-4063-3841-6   978-1-4063-5468-3

Available from all good booksellers

www.walker.co.uk